WAITING FOR ZEBRAS

Nancy Somerville

To Mum, Dad, Bill and Ritchie
with love

some people, twelve fish
ninety odd other beasties
waiting for zebras

Red Squirrel Press (Scotland)

First published in the UK 2008
By Red Squirrel Press (Scotland)
P.O.BOX 23896
Edinburgh
EH6 9AA

Red Squirrel Press (Head Office)
P.O. BOX 219 MORPETH NE61 9AU
www.redsquirrelpress.com

ISBN 978-1-906700-05-8.
Copyright The Author 2008

Printed in the UK by Athenaeum Press Ltd
Gateshead, Tyne and Wear.

Cover: Jen Rutherford.
Cover photo: Alan McGill

Contents

3

BUCKET OF FROGS

You and me
heading for the pub
in the full heat
of the mid-summer sun, then

a bucket of frogs
waiting for a bus,
that's what it looked like.
No-one else about,
just you and me
heading for the pub
and a bucket of frogs

squatting on the pavement
in the full blaze
of the mid-summer sun
- more rare in Scotland
than a bucket of frogs
taking turns to try
the high jump to freedom.

Do we leave them
to croak it
boiled in a bucket
or splattered under rubber
in Dalry Road?

Heading for the pub
with a bit of a detour
to the summer-cool canal
with a pail of hot frogs,

talking about gum trees,
other frogs we've known,
books we've read
and the things
that come to you
when you're trying to find the words
with a bucket of frogs in your hand.

Heading for the pub
with a story on our lips
- the day we saved the frogs,

and later
you saved me.

CLIMBING WITH TOMMY

Just over the next ridge,
Honest,
I lie.
Again.
But his six-year-old legs aren't persuaded
any more
by bribes of Rolos
and promises of views right over to the island,
where we camped a year ago.

-- Remember the man who broke his leg
   playing at football with us?
   And him being lifted up
   into the helicopter?
   And the way it hovered?

The distraction only works
till his sodden feet complain
and we're stuck
while he sits
stubborn in the mud.

-- Look at the snow.
And we're off again,
racing to reach the patches of white,
and I don't even mind when he stings my ear
with a direct hit.

Then the last last ridge
and he wants to know
   -- Will we really see Arran?

At the summit
it's hard to say where mists end
and clouds begin.
I'm blinded by disappointment,
but Tommy sees clearly and shouts
-- We're in the sky!
-- We're in the sky!

GULLS

I walk through tenement streets
boxed in by my life,
held in place by debts
and insecurities.

High above
a gull calls to the sea
in its sight
but distant from me

and the sound dissolves stone walls,
silences pneumatic drills.

I smell the salt,
my vision sharp
with scenes of breaking waves,
ancient rocks,
seaweed glistening
and rolling in the tide.

I see a fishing boat
with its escort of gulls,
heading for port,
past horizon islands,
hear the echo of homecoming cries.

HOME GROUND

She does not yield easily
to sight seeing
or picnic lunches,
her moods being viewed,
more often than not,
through a vague smirr
or a haar
floating like ghosts of fishermen
past windows set in stone.

She seeps through goosepimpled skin,
insinuates airways,
permeates veins
and creeps into bones
until you're part of her.

The spirit stirred on Saturday terraces
rises in the sap of rowan and gorse.
But caught in your throat
an undefinable loss
which echoes along her shores
with the oystercatcher's lament.

Your pulse is the ebb and flow
of pride and disillusionment,
the aimless lapping
of hope and regret.

BLACKBIRD

2 o'clock in the morning
and I'm walking home
alone and wishing I wasn't,
wondering why
it's always the wrong one
who drains courage
from the bottom of a glass
to make a stumbling offer
I don't want to understand.

Under Christmas lights
the streets are empty
but for me
and a solitary figure ahead,
determined on a drunken straight line.
The pavement looks as clean as a film set,
earlier rain-washed and blown-dry
ready for the night ahead.
It bounces the clicks of my heels
to the sleeping tenements
and the echo surrounds me,
too loud for comfort.

Then a blackbird sings
from a winter tree,
the joy of it so sad
it catches my throat.
I let a taxi pass.

I want to walk
and walk
to be part of the song.

BLACKBIRD 2

Heading for home
after one of those nights
when everything's gone my way.
All the right words flowed
easily and coherently
from usually tongue-tied me
and even the bar staff laughed at my jokes.

You touched my arm
as we all took our separate routes
into the darkness
and I know I'm reading too much into it,

but what the hell!
It's Spring
and there's a blackbird
singing its song again
from the graveyard trees
highlighted by orange street lamps.

A supermarket trolley stands
askew in Dalry Road
not mundane, but surreal,

and I am not vulnerable
alone in these sleeping city streets,
but head-high defiant

face the odd oncoming car,

part of the night, the song,
the life and pulse
of this place, this time.

BLACKBIRD 3
(in Glen Doll)

Does your voice have a Highland lilt
I hear but can't detect?
To me, the song is as fresh and clear
as your cousin's in Dalry Cemetery.

Its cadences and grace notes
carry through the forest,
a melody to the background theme
of rushing waters
and a chill, summer breeze
shivering leaves
as it scouts ahead for Autumn.

BLACKBURD 4

See me?
See ma voice?
See ma neck o the woods?
Miles above the rest.

See ma hen?
Sittin oan wur eggs?

A wee gem.
Keeps the nest
spick n span
an aye gies me
a wee peck oan the cheek
whin Ah get back
fae aw this territorial work
an never a peep oot o ur.

So don't mess wi me.
It's jist ma beak thit's yellae!

BLACKBIRD 5
(The Apprentice)

He's waiting in the wings,
your young rival,
thinking he can sing
with his tentative voice
jarring and discordant,
but I hear the promise.

He's probably your son,
going off half-cocked
sounding at odds
with these familiar surroundings.
But now and then
a hesitant but clear, pure note rings out
and I hear his inheritance.

As yet, your song is sure,
mellow and harmonious,

a constant thread weaving
through the story of this place.
But in his attempts
I hear your silence
in a future full of memories.

BLACKBIRD 2000

The New Year's hardly here, and already
the tinsel is losing its sparkle,

but tonight the moon presents
her own sedate eclipse display.
I open the window
to the winter chill,
as if I'll hear the music of the spheres
but instead,
voices from the street below,
too intent on conversation
to notice the silent, unhurried show.
No rocket showers or rivers of fire,
just a clear night sky,
the stars winking brighter
in compensation
as she slips behind Earth's shadow
for her subtle transformation
from pearl
to smoky topaz.

I think of my sons
as I look at the moon
- these men I taught

to say the very word,
'the cow jumped over the...?'

and I feel them moving away,
their horizons expanding.
They will sleep under strange skies,
but for now I think of them nearby
as time inexorably passes,

and the blackbird sings a lonely song.

999

The apple is in my hand
as the siren's distant sound
closes in,
responding to another
preventable tragedy.

I hold the fruit
under running water,
(which only seems pure),
and wash from its green skin
the poisons we use to kill
the poisons we perceive.

And as I bite,
chalk outlines appear
in the dust.

SKY TRAIN

Pulling out of Doncaster
under a sky red as a furnace,
the train picks up speed
and we cross blood-coloured canals
veining a landscape flat
but for lines of silhouetted trees
disappearing into the horizon.

The sky turns a brooding grey.
We pass squat towers
and tapering chimneys,
imposing their alien-ness on a wasted land,
dwarfing and diminishing all about them,
crowned by black clouds,
a pall spreading.

We leave them behind,
and the sky is fiery and wild again,
then suddenly there's an edge to it,
vermillion set against short-lived powder blue.
Canals reflect silver.

Sodium street lights glow weakly
against a cloudy grey sky
unevenly underlined
by rooftops and chimney pots.
Black box house shapes
increase in number
till we're surrounded
by city.

The engine noise quietens
to a vague rumble.
We bump and sway gently
across junctions,
slide along rails
into a waiting York.

OUR MUSIC

The party by this time
had spilled through all the flat,
wine poured in the hall, the living-room
held earnest conversations.
In the kitchen a girl cried
on more experienced shoulders,
ignored by those intent
on slices of cold pizza
and fat cigarettes.

In another room,
Thousands Are Sailing played
as we two danced
surrounded by couples
each hearing their tune,

and when our music stopped,
you kissed me softly
in the quietness.

BRIEF ENCOUNTER

Just a bit of light entertainment,
that's all it was.
An interlude of irresponsibility.
Time out from a life of pressures.

It was great while it lasted
- clichéd but true.
We pretended, you and I,
that there was no wife, no husband,
their children were not ours,
not for those hours that quickened
dead, slow weeks,
but now, when the phone rings
my first thought is that it's you.
Still.
A figure glimpsed from the bus dis
appears teasingly. A turn of
phrase overheard in the pub
causes my eyes, I know, to take on
that faraway look I always despised.

Just a bit of light entertainment.
Not serious stuff.
A passing Nancy.
That's all I was.

DEAD GULL, LOCH BRANDY

On the boulder strewn lochside
your body lies twisted,
beak open in a silent cry,
wings catching the wind
as if attempting
one last flight.

The cause of death is a mystery
to me
but nature's investigators
carry out their own post mortem,
leaving your rib cage open
to the scrutiny of the sky.

Your black beetle eye
glances my way
then crawls from the socket
revealing a skull teeming
with tiny lives.

Your feathered shroud
retains a soft and vital sheen,
its whiteness matching
the summer's persistent pockets of snow.

I rise to take my leave
and about my ears the rest of your colony
conduct a raucous consultation
on the level of my threat
to the coming generation,
now curled snug inside their shells.

The loch nestles in the corrie,
preparing for the demands
their arrival will bring.

RABBITS IN GLEN CLOVA

The hills are moving with them,
rippling,
as wave after wave
decides our presence warrants
a scurry to safety;
and what a choice of burrows
in this honeycombed glen.

We point and point
in all directions
counting and losing count
until the last white tail
bobs underground
and all is still
but for sheep
tugging at tussocks
and calling to lambs.

We turn to go, and
brown stones transform
into movement,
twitching noses appear
from behind bushes
as more and more of them
give up on concealment

and camouflage
to make a late dash
for the warren,

and as we finally leave,
the nearby rubble of an old wall
develops ears and ears
and ears.

EDINBURGH ELEPHANT

A deep grey sky
threw Scottish weather at us
and we ran for shelter
into the elephant house,
shook hair and umbrellas,
flapped coats,
flicked wrists,
sending second-hand raindrops flying
to land and be absorbed in the dust,
for the elephant house was dryness
and silence.

And when we were silent and respectful
its permanent visitor permitted us
a dry whuff from her trunk,
four dry shuffs of her feet
on straw strewn concrete.

She picked up one straw at a time
and tucked it into her mouth
--no need to speak of her dexterity,

to witness it was enough.

She walked once around the walls,
eight elephant lengths,
and stopped,
waiting we thought
for someone to open the massive sliding door
to her outside 'play' area.

We shuffled our unease
at the close-up reality
of a closed-in zoo elephant.
But we laughed our relief
as she effortlessly
elephantly
nudged aside the hanger-like door,
tested the weather with a tentative trunk,
then slammed herself in again
before turning back to us
with a deep grey sigh.

GIBBONS AT LONDON ZOO

On a platform
centre cage,
the adult gibbons hunch over
long folded legs,
chins on wrists
crossed on knees,
presenting the smallest possible target
to the London drizzle.

Their youngsters,
like all others,
ignore the weather,
playing tig around the enclosure,
custom-built for athletic apes.
Trapeze bars,
rope swings,
hoops and loops are put to use
within the bars of their playpen.
Muscles toned,
climbing skills honed
to captive perfection.

With each lap of the chase
the tarzans whoop
and swing.
A metal ring
clangs against the bars
and returns
to dunt their mother's shoulder.

She stays put, but winces

as it hits her and swings back,
she winces
as it hits her and swings back,
she winces
as it hits her and swings back,
she winces...

CUTTING MEAT

I had to stand on a stool to reach the sink.
I could only help
if I had washed properly
and used the nailbrush.

My hands must be very, very clean
so's not to spread germs
like on the TV advert,
(a wee girl in bed with a sore tummy
because her mummy hadn't been hygienic).

The slab of raw beef skirting
lies on the wooden chopping board,
yellow seams of fat
marbling the dark crimson,
glistening with freshness and blood,
smelling like nothing but itself,
sickly and dangerous.

Daddy's knife,
the one he'd used as a butcher,
is very, very sharp.

I must be careful not to cut
too close to my fingers.

The point goes in
through some resistance
then the blade pulls through the meat,
slicing a line, dividing
a small piece
off from the rest,
then again, and again,
till the whole is dismembered.

I must never, ever
put my fingers near my mouth
till I've scrubbed and scrubbed
and used the nailbrush.

SHEDDING SKINS

Eyes whitewashed
you're blind to what's before you,
your mind on a change of image
as you separate the past from your future.

When I reach out my hand
the movement has you in a sightless panic
and frantic tongue flickering
you slide back to the safety of a dark crevice.

I get the message -
PRIVATE
NO ENTRY
You're closed for redecoration,

but later, unseen
I watch
as you prepare glistening scales
for the unveiling ceremony.
You yawn abruptly   stretch   and rub
not eyes but mouth
against a stone.
An impossible smile splits your face,
widens to peel back from your head

and you emerge to leave
a skin which retains only an appearance of you.

You can discard your past,
disown it,

but I must take the husk
and put it in a box with all the others
to be brought out someday
to crumble in my hands.

(For a few days before shedding its skin, a snake's eyes cloud over,
virtually blinding it.)

THE DANCE

The music reaches peripheral tables
where we sit watching,
waiting,
wanting to join in,
enters our ears,
hearts,
and feet,
draws us together
around a pivotal point,
centripetal forces at play.

And what is The Dance?
The music is air
battered to and fro
in predetermined patterns,
the steps are tired but willing
muscles obeying
insistent electrical pulses,
the hall a compromise
between dreams

and planning regulations.

But The Dance will not submit
to reductionist dissection,
or cold logic.
Tomorrow will be time enough for blisters.

Sound and movement,
memory and emotion,
desire and pleasure,
are more than the sum of their parts.

At this gaitherin, are people,
at this *indaba*, joy,
at this ceilidh,
The Dance!

GORSE

Heading out of Oban
on the Ganavan road,
we pinch ourselves at this fourth day
of no rain, no midges,
just the thirst of a mild hangover.

All around
the gorse is bursting yellow,
fresh and vibrant as zest.
I drop back
to breathe in its creamy scent,
ancient as memory,
it takes me through the decades
to my childhood,

> holiday walks over marram-grass dunes,
> a future full of the sunshine possibilities
> of a young imagination and inexperience.

Best not to know what's ahead,
and yet,
with Mull and Kerrera
rising from a sea sparkling silver
in the early May sun,
vista of endless horizons,
what better place to be now?

I'm walking behind you,
and the way your hair curls
over your collar,
I want to touch it.

I want to just look at it,

but I slide my hand around
the nape of your neck,
kiss your ear,
caught up in that feeling
of timelessness,
urgent as Spring.

THESE WATERS

Hard to believe
the clocks go back next week,
that soon I'll be dookin for apples,
when now in Oban
the sun is hot on my cheek,
its glare on the water too bright
for my eyes, squinting at the ferry
crossing the bay from Mull.
We made that trip earlier today.

Last night, we drank in
the spirit of the place,
pointed out postcard scenes;
OK for us to sight-see in clichés
with no fish to catch, or sheep to gather,
no Beds and Breakfasts to prepare.
We think hard work's easier to bear
with such backdrops.

This morning in Craignure

a heron flapped its lazy way
along the shore to Torosay.
We heard it croak.
We *heard* the croak,

and now four swans are following
the ferry's wake,
the thwump, thwump of their slow,
heavy wingbeats
carries across the waves to shore.
Ripples spread out and return to me,

past Kerrera, Mull, Iona,
curve around Camas Tuath, Caol Ithe, Oban Bay,
these waters,
my cauldron of regeneration.

*(Dookin for apples is said to represent witches' trial by drowning,
but in more ancient times it symbolised souls in the cauldron of
regeneration.)*

EMBERS

Kneeling on your bed
we each pulled on a sweater,
more for the sake of the cold stone sill
than anything else,
and we leaned out
and breathed in
the November night.

In a garden three floors below,
a bonfire cracked
and snapped its commands
to the family who jumped when it called
but shook sparklers
in the hot face of its transience.

And as our toes rekindled flames,
our eyes followed fading smoke,
trailing into memory.

RISOTTO MARINARA

Sitting in the Europa,
grabbing a bite to eat
before I meet up with the girls,
I'm leafing through
the book I've bought,
a story-board screenplay.
Picture the scene:
        American road movie
        big desert
        red convertible
        trunk full of narcotics
cynical voice-over in my head,

then a doorful of cool night air hits me
and I look up
adjusting my perceptions...
The traffic flashing past
is keeping left,
the voices saying their good-byes are Scots,
as others calling for drinks,
the waitress is bringing my order

and the fact that it's the same dish we had
that first night
is more to do with my taste buds
and poetic licence
than any deep and meaningful desire
to be close to you through food,
isn't it? And anyway
I'm not thinking
about you at all.

WHAT I LOVE
(after Edwin Morgan)

What I love about cheese is its maturity
What I hate about adults is our blinkers
What I love about horses is their free range
What I hate about eggs is their buoyancy
What I love about the ocean is its far horizons
What I hate about distance is its sore feet
What I love about toes is their sandy beach

MENEHAM PENINSULA, FINISTERE

Barn-sized boulders
encircle us
keeping Atlantic sea-breezes at bay,

like leftovers
from a megalithic game of chuckies,
thrown from on high by cosmic giants,
their bulk used well by generations
of Breton homes
built snug
against their leeward sides.

Some of us opt for another baguette
while others drift off in ones
or twos
from the debris of our picnic.

The children, oblivious of history

and other adult affairs
go off in search of life
among the rock pools,
terrorizing crabs with monster shadows.
They uncover my memories,
snapshots of family holidays,

>Dad in canvas shoes,
>hunkered down
>pointing out velvet sea-anemones
>puckered shut in sun-warmed water.

>Mum reading in the shade,
>bare, white legs
>as unfamiliar as her inactivity.

My toe touches a shape in the sand.
I excavate a fragment of cuttlefish bone
and another
then a complete skeleton, bleached and dry;
an end more fitting
than tucked between the bars
of a suburban cage?

No trace remains of chromatophores,
its mating dance's electric colours,
pulsating lights rippling and reeling
designed to attract the right partner
at the right time.

The beach is littered
with slices and grains of immortality.
They lived, gave life,

had no inkling of their fate,
victims of time's currents.
Blind, like new lovers,
to the ripples they create,
the havoc in their wake.

FRUIT MARKETS

1.
In the shade of the gasometer
Blochairn Fruitmarket
has no place for stalls or shopping bags,
only the big boys trade here
to the noise of container lorries
backing up to loading bays.

Martha's cottage sits
an apple's throw away
in its time-warp
by the tracks of memory.

Her husband a railwayman
like his father, son and grandson,
but early graves and redundancy
made a mockery of tradition.

A widow now,
afraid to go out,
afraid to come home
again to find her bags of flour
thrown at walls

by hands that never held home-baking,
her carpet sticky with sugar,
piles of human shite in each room,
left by apprentices of housebreaking.

2.
Music and ordered words compete gently
with the clink of cappuccino cups
and bottles of imported lagers.

The Gallery's whitewashed iron beams
are heavy with history.
Did its builders dream of poems
recited under their hammered work?
To the rhythm of their blows
were symphonies composed?
Only the rivets know.

3.
The orange-tops park side by side.

This stop on our itinerary
is the ancient covered market
where countless kilos of Breton apples
were polished and sniffed,
their potential for cidre assessed,

but this is not market day
so the talk is of whether to stay here
to while away the midday quiet
or pick up bottled water,
camera films,
and head for Carnak's standing stones.

The decision passes me by.

I can only think of you,
and her,
sighing over a map,
planning a journey
with no place for gooseberries.

(Lothian Regional Council minibuses, with white body work and orange roofs, were known as 'orange tops'.)

WILD GEESE FLYING SOUTH

I watch the dark skein swerve and wheel
and return to its purpose,
each bird defined
against a misty, grey sky.

The rain-stained glass
and traffic noise
keep me from their calls,
and I feel apart
from life itself.
Rhythms and drives
are sanitised and commodified
rituals removed
more and more
from root and purpose.

The outstretched necks

and curves of wings
are living shorthand messages
for those, like me,
without direction,
left behind
to the hard shoulders and cold hearts
of a lost people.

ON THE BUS (1988)

My smile is at first indulgent,
a bit smug even,
as behind me on the bus
an amiable drunk
remarks on the comings and goings,
     - C'moan oan hen, therr's a seat.
      Ye nearly missed yur stoap son.
      Get doon the sterrs ya black bastart!

Someone giggles and he laughs,
responding to the acknowledgement,
but a young girl's voice,
the one that leaves the rest of us
relieved and ashamed, says,
     - That's no funny.

So he stops laughing,
but armed with our sins of omission
proclaims,
     - If this wiz South Africa
      she widnae even be allowed oan.

Then, before lapsing into silence,
this bairn of Jock Tamson sings
The Sash and shouts
          - Fuck the Pope!
just to round things off.

It could almost be funny;
is he wondering who next to insult?
I prepare my cutting comment
for when I'll have to pass him,

but rising and turning,
find the bus is full of faces
and I can't tell which is his.

HAAR

This time we argue in the pub,
both thinking, 'This is over nothing'.
I know this because I know you.
Leaving my drink to show my hurt,
I join the lonely night.

Words used to be easy keys
opening us to each other.
Words now are looming, widening walls
with no way around or through.

The chilling haar envelops me
strips me raw
of any pretence of pride.

CORIOLIS

This sky above me
is also over Camas,
where the rising tide
divides and unites around
ever diminishing rocks,
where sea, hills and sky meet
to form angles of elements
reaching out to infinity,

but I'm here in rush hour traffic
looking up from long shadows
to where the early evening light
sets ablaze the wings of pigeons
homing in on city rooftops
-- a flock of glitter spiralling
in ever-decreasing circles,
surrendering to the coriolis effect,
drawn to their earth.

THE LAST SWIFT

Each Spring,
faithfully, I record in my diary
the date the first swift arrives,
all the way from Africa
to these uncertain skies.

My Summers
are filled with their presence,
the wheeling cries
diving through tenement canyons,
the boomerang shapes
rising to invisibility.

Every Autumn
I miss the date
the last swift leaves
and I wonder
if this slow dawning of absence
is how it will be
with our last kiss.

END OF THE AFFAIR

You've been around
for close to half a century
and think you've seen everything
this life has to offer,
then one black night
you glimpse
the mirror of the window
just as beams of headlights
glance off raindrops
held in brief suspension
on the glass,

and suddenly
it's a tinsel show from Christmas past
when glitter and tricks
were laid on for your pleasure
as you clapped hands
and laughed your delight at the pretence.

It's the oldest cliché in the book;
finding out he's married
all along.
But this time the wedding
was halfway through the illicit affair
you hadn't a clue you were having,

and even at your age
you can't escape the irony
that it's him you want
to hold you and kiss away
the pain he's caused.

The magic goes from the glass
and you're left with no illusions,
just reflections
in the streaks of rain.

DEPARTURES

Waiting for the bus
this August morning
to take me to the work
I've lost all interest in,

familiar landmarks,
touchstones, have gone.

The future has changed,
the departures board shuddering
with all the implications
of your leaving.

I look up to the blue sky,
see swifts massing,
for their yearly exile.

Summer's over.

BEST BEFORE

I feel Autumn approach,
a change in the air,
the quality of light,
a realisation that shivers will betray
any brightness to come.

Summer's golden days
are scenes from another life,
filled with hot kisses,
sleepy morning reachings
and promises of forever
dropping from your lips

like shiny red apples
rotting from within,
only good
for worm food.

LAST KISS

I *do* remember our last kiss.

You lying back on the bed,
I showered and fresh
stretching across to grab my clothes,
and as your mouth searched out mine,
straddled you,
turning my back
to the dark clouds
gathering over the Sound of Mull.

IN THE BALMORAL

One o'clock Saturday,
SCOTLAND v ENGLAND.

As the team lists replace Braveheart
on the big screen
someone shouts
       - Aw, hey! Ah've no seen that.
       - D'ye want me tae tell ye the endin?
says Andy behind the bar,
but already he's complaining
about Craig Brown's selection.

I'm the only woman here, and yet,
could stand naked on the bar
- Christ, so could Posh Spice!
and all eyes would still be on her man

doing his best to spoil our day.

Where now is the sexual imperative?
Lost its way
up the competition cul-de-sac
where our males display vicariously.
Are we meant to be impressed?
Figure out somehow their genes
are as good as their team's?

Still,
at least there's no queue
in the ladies.

IN THE KEEL ROW

The two collies
keep their bodies low to the ground,
alert for any movement,
eyes on the drinkers standing at the bar
or sitting by the blazing November fire.

A shuffled foot
cocks their ears,
a waving hand
tenses them to readiness.

Someone stands,
makes a break for the bar.
The dogs work as a team,

one each side
rounding up the stray,
herding him back
to his place,
three pints in his hands.

Then, flock settled,
they crouch
on guard again,
ready to nip
any more displays of individuality
in the bud.

CORNCRAKE ON IONA

Their call is the sound my alarm clock makes
as I turn its key to set the time
but it's me who's being wound up.

I hear it all around
in that field, this garden
then just ahead
now right beside me
from those reed beds.

I feign indifference, striding on,
slow down,
look and look
but the birds elude me,

or is it just one,

throwing its voice,
scuttling behind me
while my bins are trained on a likely hummock?

Is it a VisitScotland conspiracy?
I imagine speakers hidden in ditches,
triggered by unseen pressure pads,

then a brazen bird is pointed out
by a fellow victim
(or Tourist Board plant),
at the crossroads in full sunlight
bold in short grass,
for maximum effect,

sounding the alarm
to the world at large:
I'm here! I'm here!
Crex! Crex!

SHEEP

No free thinkers here.
We go with the flock,
never stick our scrag ends out,
always do what's expected of us.

Who needs freedom
when we've this whole field to ourselves?
There's nothing out there
but wolves and rogue lambs
bleating on
about democracy and free speech,
not to mention vegetarianism.
Well, we don't care what anyone says,
one shepherd's much the same as any other
and they know what's best for us.

What's wrong with woolly thinking?
It keeps us snug and smug.
We know our place.
If we've done nothing wrong
we've nothing to worry about.
Right?

SCOTLAND / ALBA

A parliament reconvened,
both shadow and vigorous shoot
of its former self.
The old syzygy of the national psyche
lifts a finger in encouragement and warning
to those who stayed and exiles returning;
Darien survivors,
Marbella's Big Tam, Big Macs,
iMacs and Cape Breton pipers,
diaspora back from New Zealand / Aotearoa,

and even Westminster.

DAVID PATERSON FORD (1808 - 1871)

My great-great-grandfather,
an Auchtermuchty weaver,
died there
in the wee small hours
of a chill December morning.

There's a note of accusation
on the death certificate:
Found dead in a dog cart...
supposed to be heart disease,
no medical attendant.

I hear the, *Aye rights!*
gossip at the looms,
the stories woven
as nimble fingers worked,

as his were frozen to the reins.

RE-GENERATIONS
(Agnes Paton: 1886-1964)

Yellow may my butter be, firm and round;
Thy breasts are sweet, firm, round and sweet.
So may my butter be, Bridget, sweet.
- Hebridean Invocation to Bride

My granny was born on St Bride's Day,
Imbolc, when milk comes into ewes,
and the adder slides from under its stone
to greet the warmth of the first Spring day.

Her favourite food was Bride's broth,
a mound of milky, mashed potato,
a knob of creamy butter on top.

They called her Agnes,
the lamb,
and her daughter was Agnes too
and I am named for both of them.

Granny'd been a widow six months
when I was born. My mother said
I gave her a reason to go on.
New life after a bitter winter.

SMIDDY

A huge open doorway
into a barn of a place,
alive with fiery shadows.

I cling to my father's hand,
torn between its security
and the fear of going with him
to the source of the mysteries.

The man in the long leather apron
seemed unconcerned
by the molten fire
sparking and spitting to be free.

"I've brought the wee one to see the horses."
The smith nods,
waves us nearer the anvil.

The horses.

One chestnut giant
pulls back from the man
at its head
while another stamps impatience
from the darkness.

Both riderless,
like the untamed mustangs in my book.

Their big smell envelops me,
their audible breath
seems hotter than the forge.
The reflection of its glow
pulses on their flanks.

So much animal
with no cage between us.

"D'ye want tae clap them, hen?
Thull no touch ye."

But it's too late.

BROTHER

That night we couldn't have our own display,
you took me round Ruchazie's bonfires.

Mum told you to look after me,
made me promise to hold your hand
and did I understand that if I wasn't good
you'd bring me right back?

I mind that first we went to Billy Shaw's,
your red-haired pal who never spoke to me.
You talked your strange teenage boy talk
in the stairwell,
as I stood,
impatient for the fireworks I could hear us missing,
but silent and still in case this was a test.

At last, your conversation ended,
he closed his door.
I grasped your hand as we descended,
eager to get out and into the night.
We walked past gaps in fences
where palings once stood,
ripped out by the boys
who'd raided and guarded
their pile of fuel for weeks.

No need for Mum's warnings;
I was too afraid of the darkness
to leave your side,
too mesmerised by crackling fires
and whirling sparks,
too aware of this adventure
with a brother I idolised,
to think of doing a thing
that would make me even smaller
in your eyes.

I must have felt and smelled the too-close fires,
piled high with wood, armchairs
and the odd pathetic Guy,
must have seen the rockets, heard their rising hiss,
and surely jumped as bangers echoed,

but what I remember through the haze of years
is rows of bonfires under a smoky, starry sky,
Galdenoch Street unfamiliar in an orange, shadowy glow

and a glimpse of growing up,

feeling safe and protected
as everything around me exploded.

MOTHER

Did I ever tell you
how safe and loved I felt
walking up that quiet road
in the dark, alone,
when I saw you silhouetted
in the triangle of light
as you held back the curtain
watching for my safe return?

Now that *I* lie listening
for my son's key in the lock
I understand your fears for me.
Now *I* feel the horror
of a thousand dreadful ends,
the shiver the morning headline sends.

TO KENDRA

When I was young
the lark rose on its song
trilled out of sight
and I was
daughter
sister
grandchild in white angora.

When I was young
the water's edge boiled
with tadpoles
eager for jam jars
and I had parents
illusions
all my teeth.

When I was young
old old people died
and children
in countries far far away
and guilt was for
an unwashed face
a broken vase
a cross-my-heart lie.

Around the corner
when I was young,
endless fields
a boundless loch
all the time in the world.

SONNET FOR STEVEN

When word came through that you'd been born
my friends and I had met
to sow seeds for a new dawn
- naive perhaps, and yet
who else has ever changed the world
but dreamers with more hope than sense
destined to be ridiculed
by those who view through cynicism's lens.

Our tiny slice of space and time's unique
- there is no second chance.
We take a leap of faith and seek
solutions, or give in to circumstance.
On your first night, clouds parted to reveal
stars out of reach but none the less quite real.

SKY DIVER

His element is air.

Positioning his body
to manoeuvre as he wills,
his aim to stay suspended there,
in the company of gulls,
resisting gravity.

Training kicks in
and, altitude checked,
he pulls the cord

and the opening chute tugs,
buffeted by high winds,
slowing his descent so rapidly
it feels like he's climbing
back to the heights,

but he's dropping
fast, towards the hard ground;
has been from the moment
he stepped into thin air.

No gentle drifting
but a rush to land,
with skill, on his feet,
gathering up the billows.
Even now he's planning the next jump,

as his mother offers up
another silent prayer of thanks.

SUMMIT OF SNOWDON

We wear the mist
like a chilling layer,
peering through it
at each other.

We could be anywhere
or nowhere,
just the trig point solid
between us,
something to hold onto
as the wind pushes and tugs,
snatches our voices away.

One step
and you disappear.
I'm surrounded by nothing
but grey.

A gull and its calls drift in
and out of the world.

THIS SMALL WORLD

It's not yet midnight
and for once
my sons are home,
safe in their beds,

but no room for complacency
in this small world.
Bombs drop through the dark
like waking nightmares
into the *Land of Suffering and Sorrow*.
A fine dust lies
on New York doormats,
ready for fingers of suspicion,

and now, outside my window,
battle cries and siren wails
as the leisure complex spills
out-of-their-heads teenagers
onto the streets,

but for this night at least,
I lie in uneasy content.
My sons are safe asleep,
my roof intact.

(Afghanistan is known as 'the Land of Suffering and Sorrow')

UNKNOWN SOLDIER

In the pile of photos of Edinburgh's past,
Cox's Glue Works, the Snow White laundry,
coopers and souters at their crafts,
I come across you, posed in a studio,
from a sepia time.

Your eyes speak to me
with an expression close to home,
like my adolescent son,
embarrassed to be at the centre of things.
You stand at gawky attention,
all set for the trenches
in your stiff army uniform,
an awkward smile on your face,
and slow burning terror
in your teenage eyes.

I can tell you're overwhelmed by events,
wondering how this happened.
You believed the Kitchener posters,
carried along by the bravado of your friends.
Were you your mother's little soldier
when she bathed a skint knee?
Surely she cried to see her boy
set out for a war beyond her arms
and soothing words.

I think you were shy,
not especially of note,

not too clever, or good at sport,
trying to prove you too were special,
like a story-book hero
with a town to liberate.

I'll never know your name
or what was your fate
but when the call comes
for more sacrifice
I wonder why we never learn
from your bewildered eyes.

GODDESS

She dazzles with terrible light
and yet
her dimpled, eternally open arms
welcome all.

Her passion burns
with tigress ferocity
yet weeping
she dries the world's tears.

Her beauty terrifies,
yet her smile is your mother's
cradling and crooning a lullaby.

An eider-down diamond,

a porridge sword,
a flame of snow,
she embraces contradiction.

Young as innocence,
fecund as the Earth,
ancient as nothing.

PRIMARY COLOURS

There are fish swimming in the sky
in the Primary 3 Dali on the wall.
Autumn leaves mutate into halibuts.
A codling calls, 'Hello' to a passing haddock.
Puffer fish fall from kelp trees
past an unmistakable blackbird
heading for star fish
in the mackerel sky.

INDIAN SUMMER

Late September
and the graveyard trees
are still heavy
with the fruits of their year's labour,
swaying ponderously
in the wake of a balmy evening breeze.

A gap in the traffic exposes the silence,
no birdsong,
no footballing voices,
just an expectant hush
as Autumn holds her breath
gathering strength
for sap-scaring frost,
leaf-whipping gales,
the snowploughs of winter.

JERVIS BAY, NEW SOUTH WALES

Cradled in southern waters,
I float in the gentle tide,
sunlit dapples glint the surface.

I'm dazzled
by the fierce beauty of this land.
As if through a dream
I watch loved ones
wander on the whitest sands
framed by eucalyptus trees.

Later we'll all be there
at the beach wedding,
the reason we're here;
this is a time
and a place for new beginnings,
a rebirth perhaps.

My hand trawls the seabed
scoops fistfuls of shimmering sand.
I must grasp life again,
stop this drifting,
letting everything slip
through my fingers.

IN AUSTRALIA

This country
doesn't usually do things by half.
Its Barrier Reef,
like its Sandy Desert,
is Great.

At the zoo
we'd seen the platypus swim
even glimpsed the echidna
(the world's only monotremes).

The most venomous jellyfish,
spiders and snakes
on the planet lurk here
but it wasn't one of them
that got the quoll.

Near the World's Steepest Railway,
halfway down the Giant Staircase
we stopped for a rest
in the wettest rain I've known
(and I'm Scottish).

Then, under a eucalypt,
white polka dots
on chocolate brown fur,
a tail, two legs,
a bit of belly.

Undoubtedly,
half a quoll.

GUID NYCHBURRIS, DUMFRIES

A hundred horses are clattering
up Bank Street,
tearing past Ladbrokes,
riders ululating
like a Bedouin hen party.

The punters inside
have their heads down,
studying.
Horses, to them,
are starting times and form,
flimsy pink slips,
a short-cut to a week's wages,
if they're lucky.

Outside in the flesh,
in lathered sweat,
nostrils stretched open,
eyes rolling,
the beasts strain against the reins,
prance like prima donnas,
skittish on the cobbles,
hemmed in by the narrowing vennel.
The yelling, waving crowds
cheer them on,

but wary of their power
are weighing up the odds
of a kick in the teeth.

PASITHEA CALE EUPHROSYNE
(The Three Graces)

Your marble lips are sealed;
no gossips,
you keepers of ancient secrets,
self-contained, content in your trinity.
Three in one, you've spanned the globe,
names changing with time's tides
-- *Brilliant, Flowering, Heart's Joy*
-- *Faith, Hope, Charity.*

I circle your pedestal searching for clues,
can't but compare your firm perfection
to my hot-flush flesh, slave to gravity,
envy your embrace of kinship and love,
immortal moment of suspension.

At night,
when the gallery's silent and dark,
you tiptoe down and, holding hands,
dance around and through the rooms,
call 'Good Hunting' to Diana's nymphs,
coo to the baby, asleep by the roses,
laugh at mortals whose hours are past,
and lastly, pause by Venus,
-- *Aphrodite, Goddess of Joy, Beautiful to All*
-- let us in,

then sighing, drift back,
arrange your modest drapes,
prepare for the cold day.

PRINCES STREET

Heading for the bus
after a long, hard day
when a piper tunes up
then the Mingulay Boat Song
carries me
from conveyer-belt cars
and the empty busyness of the city
to where big skies
and wee shops
leave space for life's essentials,

and seeing my smile mirrored
in the faces of fellow travellers,
is some comfort
in this crowded loneliness.

MINK AT CAMAS

A golden light spreads over the bay
as the long, hot day
melts into evening.
The oyster-catchers make another low-flying pass,
their familiar piping chorus links
my memories to this moment.

A pair of mink move over the rocks
like shadows
or a trick of light
till one abruptly scoops a crab
from a shallow pool,
crunching with relish
and noisy carelessness,
then slips into the water
following her mate
swimming for the opposite shore,

and for a time
there is only the lapping of the incoming tide,
making gentle but unrelenting demands
on brittle seaweed
and sun-warmed sand.

1ST JULY 1999

(1) The Mornin

Auld Andrew stauns next tae us
in the Royal Mile.
His chin bristles
wi quite a few days growth.
He's seen better days,
n'younger days,
a bit threadberr,
lik his coat.
He points up tae the Saltire
flappin in a wee breeze
above the City Chambers,
      That's ma flag!
he tells anybuddy thit's listnin,
then, as the Black Watch march past
fur aboot the thurd time this mornin,
he whips aff his bunnit
stauns tae attention'n salutes.
      They're aw here, he saiz
      The Marines, the Raff, the Ermy.
      Whutz evrybuddy waitin fur?
Naebuddy answers.

Who knows why anybuddy's here?
The spectacle?
The historicity?
The rerr sunshine?
Some are tourists,
nae denyin it,
but some are locals

thit've hud tae skive aff work
fur it's no a public holiday,
(surely shum mishtake).

They're mibbe here tae see thit
oor elected representatives
keep their noses clean,
an know their place,
lik the Newhaven wifies
thit yaised tae fling fish
it the Commissioners
o the auld parliament
if they didnae like
whut they wur gettin up tae.

There are mibbe even a few royalists here,
but the muted response fae the crowd
whin Lizzie, Chooky'n Chuck eventually pass
disnae jist reflect
the 'Culture o Silence' in this land,
fur whin the street sweepers come by,
pushin their trolleys,
clearin up efter the hoarses,
the biggest cheer o the mornin goes up,
an it's obvious thit people
are wantin tae make a point.

The sweepers gie a royal wave
wae their shovels
an the crowd yells even louder.

A voice saiz
          Ah luv this country.

(2) The Efternin

Sittin in Milne's Bar
we raise a glass
tae the new parliament;
fur some a haufwye hoose,
fur others nothin but crumbs fae the table
tae shut us up,
an mibbe fur a few, a step too faur.
But wan thing Ah'm sure o
- somethin hud tae chynge.

Ah look up tae meet
MacCaig's piercin eyes,
turn an see MacDiarmid's
interrogatin glower,
an the enormity o the day
hits me again;
whin Ah think thit they missed it
bi so narra a margin...

But mibbe no
fur oor past is in oor present
an the school weans
merchin doon The Mound
wi their banners,
an pipin up a storm wi Martyn Bennett
in the Gerdens,
gie us hope fur the future;
Scotland playin a tune,
rooted in the wealth o oor traditions
growin an reachin oot tae ithers
wi the confidence

tae make somethin new aw thegither.

(3) Reality Check

Wanderin roon the toon,
soakin in the perty mood
alang wi the heat an light beamin doon
fae a sky still clear o clouds,
we bump into friends
thit campaigned wi us,
marched, grett an yearned fur this day,
yet we know thit politicians
have short memories
- they're already startin tae say
it wiz them thit made it happen.

We come hame tae get chynged,
fur thenight's celebrations
n'catch the TV news,
n'Ah don't know whither tae laugh
or throw the shoe Ah'm takin aff
whin Ah see thit they've matched
the cheers fur the street sweepers
wi the footage o the royal carriage.

(4) The Big Hooley

In the Assembly Rooms
the Music Hall's goat
traditional tunes,
movin, fit-tappin, beautiful

in turn,
an there are people sittin listnin
at tables, oan the flerr
or jist staunin at the back.

Ah stood next tae David Steel,
an didnae realise
tae Ah turned roon.
But the night
maist people want tae dae somethin,
tae dance,
an celebrate,
so here across the hallway
the room swirls
tae the Fish Band,
kilts, skirts, troosers, shorts,
even the odd ball gown
twirlin an birlin in time tae the music
lik a shoal turnin as wan
in the ocean's currents.

Ah've jist met John Swinney,
danced wi another MSP;
Hell, evrybuddy in the room huz,
an Ah'm thinkin o auld Edinburgh
n'how aw the classes
yaised tae live'n work'n eat
cheek bi jowl,
crammed alang the spine
o the auld toon.

Then Cathy Peattie
gets oan stage wi the band

n'sings the 'Freedom Come All Ye',
wi a voice so strong'n true
thit yi wonder if the Parliament
should really be her day joab.
The crowd staun
an a lot jine in,
the ithers wishin they knew the words.
Ah kin hardly get thum past
the lump in ma throat,

n'Ah think o ma sons
n'the rest o their generation
doon in the Gerdens
listnin tae Shirley Manson an Garbage
n'Ah know they'll be huvin
jist as good a time as Ah um,
n'Ah know they can ceilidh
wi the best o thum,

fur this country isnae wan culture,
or class,
we're no wan generation,
or gender,
we've goat merr thun wan language,
an strings tae wur bow,
we're each o us bits o awthings,
wi as many moods n'aspects
as the weather,
an as lang as we remember
tae celebrate that
wull be fine.

Acknowledgements

With thanks to the editors of the following anthologies, magazines and newspapers in which versions of some of these poems have appeared:

Rich Pickings (Poetry Now, 1991), *Past Dancing* (Central Writers, 1992), *The Coracle* (Iona Community, 1993, 1999), *Spread the Words* (Adult Learning Project, 1995), *Pushing the Boat Out* (Wild Goose Publications, 1995), *The Ice Horses* (Scottish Cultural Press, 1996), *A New Beginning* (Brown and Whittaker Publishing, 1999), *Poetry Scotland* (1999), *The Herald* (1999), *Edinburgh: An Intimate City* (City of Edinburgh Council, 2000), *Such Strange Joy* (iynx, 2001), *Elephant's Eye* (Diggers Writers, 2002), *The World & Elsewhere* (RookBook Publications, 2002), *Sand* (2003), *Markings* (2003), *The Flow: Poetry from Camas* (Rachel McCann Publishing, 2003), *Candles & Conifers* (Wild Goose Publications, 2005), *Close Encounters* (Diggers Writers, 2005), *100 Favourite Scottish Poems* (Luath Press, 2006), *There's a Poem to be Made* (Shore Poets, 2006), *Skein of Geese* (Stanza, 2007), *Brighid's Runes* (Mica Arts, 2008), *Bucket of Frogs: NWS 26* (ASLS 2008)

Thanks also to members of Central, ALP and WEA Diggers writers groups for advice, support, friendship and pints over the years, to Jen Rutherford for her time and hard work, Kevin Cadwallender for persevering, Sheila Wakefield from Red Squirrel Press for having faith in me.

Love and gratitude to Graham and Alan for putting up with me and all the ancient computers, to family and friends for their support - you know who you are.

Finally, I'd like to acknowledge the encouragement of the late Mark Ogle who first suggested I could be a writer, and of the late Bryan Astor who kept telling me to hurry up with this collection.